YOKO Finds Her Way

ROSEMARY WELLS

Disney • HYPERION BOOKS
NEW YORK

One day an envelope with two tickets arrived in the mail.
"Tomorrow, my little cherry blossom," said Yoko's mama,
"we are going to fly all the way to Japan!"

"Can Miki come too?" asked Yoko.

"Of course," said Yoko's mama.

That night Yoko and Miki packed their suitcases.

Yoko and her mama put their suitcases in the car.
"Could you read the signs for me?" said Yoko's mama.

Yoko saw the sign for the airport.
"Turn here, Mama!" said Yoko.

Left turn was Rising Sun Airways. "No!" said Yoko.

Right turn was Air Palm. "No!" said Yoko.

Straight ahead was Big Wave Airlines. "Go!" said Yoko.

"Parking this way, Mama!" said Yoko.

"You are my helpful cherry blossom!" said Yoko's mama.

"Luggage cart over here, and Air Train that way, Mama!"

Yoko and her mama stood in line. They showed their passports.
They emptied their handbags and took off their shoes.
Even Miki had to go through the X-ray machine.

When it was all over, Yoko's mama said, "I am exhausted!"
"Tea, Mama! Right over there!" said Yoko.

Yoko and her mama found Gate 54.
They found tea for Mama and ice cream for Yoko.

Soon there was sticky red-bean ice cream all over Yoko.
"I'll wash up in the Big Girls' room, Mama," said Yoko.
But Yoko's mama had fallen fast asleep.

Yoko knew which bathroom was which.
It was easy. There were signs.
Yoko found the soap.

She turned on the water and then the Paw Dryer.
Clean and dry, she went back to her mama.
But Yoko went out the wrong door.

Outside, there was no Mama.

There was no Gate 54, and no Big Wave.

Yoko was in the middle of Air Palm.

"Now I am in big trouble!" said Yoko.

Yoko stepped onto an escalator.
Big Wave and Gate 54 were nowhere to be seen.
"Mama!" cried Yoko.

Yoko followed the signs to the Airport Police and asked for help.

"Of course I will help you!" said the police lady.

"That is what I'm here for!"

She blew her whistle, and a speedy cart zipped up to them. Yoko and the police lady rode all the way back to Gate 54, Big Wave Airlines.

But there was no Mama waiting there!
Yoko's mama was looking for Yoko in the washroom.

GATE F 7836

Mama went through another wrong door. She was in the middle of Rising Sun Airlines. "I am in big trouble!" said Yoko's mama.

Yoko's mama took the moving walkway to the Food Court.
"Yoko!" she cried. Tears streamed down her cheeks.
"Where are you, Yoko?"

The pizza chef and the hot dog chef offered comfort food.

But Yoko's mama did not want to eat.

"I just want my baby!" she said.

An Air Palm pilot offered to help.

A Rising Sun flight attendant brought her tea.

Together they walked Yoko's mama all the way back

to Gate 54 in the Big Wave terminal, where Yoko waited.

"Mama!" cried Yoko.

"My little cherry blossom!" shouted Yoko's mama.

"Boarding Flight Six to Japan!" said a voice on the loudspeaker.

"Do you know which way to go?" asked Yoko's mama.

"Just follow me!" said Yoko. "I'm following the signs!"

For information address Disney • Hyperion Books, 125 West End Avenue, New York, New York 10023.
First Edition
10 9 8 7 6 5 4 3 2 1
H106-9333-5-13288
Printed in Malaysia
Library of Congress Cataloging-in-Publication Data
Wells, Rosemary.
Yoko finds her way / Rosemary Wells.—First edition.
pages   cm
Summary: When Yoko gets lost in the airport, she uses her sign-reading skills to find her way back to her mama.
ISBN 978-1-4231-6512-5
[1. Airports—Fiction. 2. Signs and signboards—Fiction. 3. Lost children—Fiction.
4. Japanese Americans—Fiction. 5. Cats—Fiction.] I. Title.
PZ7.W46843Yof 2014   [E]—dc23   2012027565

Designed by Joann Hill
The art was created using gouache and collage.
The type was set in 20-point Goudy Old Style.
Reinforced binding
Visit www.disneyhyperionbooks.com